MW00903112

A blessing especially for

_____

A Blessing for
WINTER'S
CHILD

Words by PETER
HINCKLEY

BUSHEL
& PECK
BOOKS

*D*earest child of winter,
may the magic of your
season always live within you.

May each day be as
wondrous as the
newly fallen snow...

. . . as joyful as the angels . . .

. . . and as warm as the
copper kettle.

$\mathcal{M}$ay the winter wind be
ever at your back . . .

...the sun warm
upon your face...

... and the snow soft
beneath your feet.

*M*ay you soar like the cardinal through life's wintry sunshine...

... run like the deer in
its frosted forests ...

...bend like the birch when its winds blow...

... and always have the strength
of the ancient oak, who knows
that no storm lasts forever.

*M*ay you
always be
filled with the
magical warmth that
is your season . . .

. . . of yule logs . . .

...of candlelight...

. . . of stars that
shine in an
indigo sea.

*M*ay all of
winter
remind you
what a joy you
are to the world!

The birds that sing for you . . .

...the lights that leap for you...

...the white that gleams for you...

...the flakes that
dance with delight at
the very mention of
your name.

May all your days burst with the joy and color that are your birthright to have:

The red of the holly, to
remind you to stand out.

The orange
of the sun, to
remind you to be
a light to others.

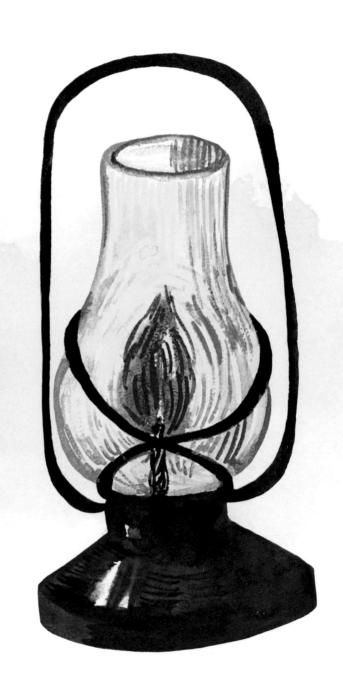

The yellow of the flame,
to remind you to dance.

The green of the
pine, to remind you
to stand tall.

The blue of the ice, to
remind you to sparkle.

The violet of the mountains,
to remind you to be true to
the royal within.

For you, child of winter,
    are all that is good, all that
is bright, all that is beautiful
in this magical time of year.

*A*nd that makes you special, indeed.

ABOUT BUSHEL & PECK BOOKS

Bushel & Peck Books is a children's publishing house with a special mission. Through our Book-for-Book Promise™, we donate one book to kids in need for every book we sell. Our beautiful books are given to kids through schools, libraries, local neighborhoods, shelters, nonprofits, and also to many selfless organizations that are working hard to make a difference. So thank you for purchasing this book! Because of you, another book will make its way into the hands of a child who needs it most.

If you liked this book, please leave a review online at your favorite retailer. Honest reviews spread the word about Bushel & Peck—and help us make better books, too!

NOMINATE A SCHOOL OR ORGANIZATION TO RECEIVE FREE BOOKS

Do you know a school, library, or organization that could use some free books for their kids? We'd love to help! Please fill out the nomination form on our website (see below), and we'll do everything we can to make something happen.

www.bushelandpeckbooks.com/pages/
nominate-a-school-or-organization

BUSHEL
& PECK
BOOKS

Copyright © 2022 by Peter Hinckley.

Published by Bushel & Peck Books, a family-run publishing house
in Fresno, California, that believes in uplifting children with the
highest standards of art, music, literature, and ideas. Find beautiful
books for gifted young minds at www.bushelandpeckbooks.com.

Type set in Aunt Mildred and IM Fell English Pro

Artwork licensed from Shutterstock.com

Bushel & Peck Books is dedicated to fighting illiteracy all over the
world. For every book we sell, we donate one to a child in need—
book for book. To nominate a school or organization to receive free
books, please visit www.bushelandpeckbooks.com.

ISBN: 9781638195009

First Edition

Printed in the United States

10 9 8 7 6 5 4 3 2 1